THE MOST MAGNIFICENT IDEA

For anyone who has ever stared helplessly at a blank page

Published in Canada and the U.S. by Kids Can Press Ltd.
25 Dockside Drive, Toronto, ON M5A 0B5

Kids Can Press is a Corus Entertainment Inc. company
www.kidscanpress.com

The art in this book was rendered digitally in Photoshop after repeated room tidyings, many hours staring out of the window and one existential crisis.

The text is set in Bookeyed Nelson.

Edited by Yasemin Uçar
Designed by Karen Powers

Printed and bound in Shenzhen, China, in 3/2022 through Asia Pacific Offset

CM 22 0 9 8 7 6 5 4 3 2 1

FSC
www.fsc.org
MIX
Paper from
responsible sources
FSC® C012521

LIBRARY AND ARCHIVES CANADA CATALOGUING IN PUBLICATION

Title: The most magnificent idea / written and illustrated by Ashley Spires.

Names: Spires, Ashley, 1978– author, illustrator.

Identifiers: Canadiana 20210342196 | ISBN 9781525305047 (hardcover)

Classification: LCC PS8637.P57 M677 2022 | DDC jC813/.6 — dc23

Kids Can Press gratefully acknowledges that the land on which our office is located is the traditional territory of many nations, including the Mississaugas of the Credit, the Anishnabeg, the Chippewa, the Haudenosaunee and the Wendat peoples, and is now home to many diverse First Nations, Inuit and Métis peoples.

We thank the Government of Ontario, through Ontario Creates; the Ontario Arts Council; the Canada Council for the Arts; and the Government of Canada for supporting our publishing activity.

THE MOST MAGNIFiCENT IDEA

Written and illustrated by

Ashley Spires

KIDS CAN PRESS

This is a regular girl and her best friend in the whole wide world. They do all kinds of things together. They play. They cuddle. They daydream. And they make things.

Well, SHE makes things.

The girl builds cozy things, whirling things
and helpful things ...

things that grow, things that float
and things that swing.

Some of her creations are good ...

some are great ...

and a few are even MAGNIFICENT.

Her brain is an idea machine.

It's so full of ideas that her hands can barely keep up.

Every morning begins with a snuggle and a stretch, and then she's ready to build.

But today feels different.
She has her supplies
and her assistant, but
something is missing ...

The girl has never NOT had an idea before.

But that's okay, ideas can't be that hard to find.

Going for a walk is a good place to start.
Her assistant heartily agrees.

They stroll and skip and
play and splash.

They admire other builders at work.

And they help out a friend.

There you are! You're not
supposed to be outside.

The girl returns to her workshop, but still no idea.
She looks around for inspiration ...

She could build a mobile, but she's already made four of those.
Or some cat toys for the neighbor, but she made a boxful last week.

She could make a fort, dog stairs, a bookshelf or
a solar-heated birdhouse, but those are OLD ideas.
She needs a NEW idea.

A MAGNIFICENT
new idea!

She flips through her notebooks.

She brainstorms with a friend.

She researches the greats.

She digs through her entire house, but she can't find a single idea anywhere.

She decides to start making something —
anything — without having an idea first.

zzzzzzzzzz

When she's finished, she steps back to see ...

Well, let's just say it's not her best work.

Maybe she needs a break
from making things. She'll do
something different today.

She tries a bunch of new activities.
But they are all too dangly,
too dizzy, too noisy ...

too buggy, too soggy and too slow.

Enough is ENOUGH. The girl MUST get a new idea.
She will not move until she thinks of something.

She sits. She stares.

She waits for an idea to pop into her head.

But all the waiting makes her grouchy.

ARGH!
She needs to get out.
She needs to explore.
She needs to discover ...

DIFFERENT
SUPPLIES!

The girl finds bits, bobs and thingamajigs, but no ideas. Why is this so hard?!

She makes things — it's what she does!
So WHY can't she just make an IDEA?

She shuts her eyes, plugs her ears and holds
her breath to FORCE an idea into her brain.

When that doesn't work, she tries jumping up and down on one foot to shake an idea loose.

She tries standing on her head, doing cartwheels ... and clucking like a chicken.

BAGAWK!

Without ideas taking up space, her brain fills up with sad instead.

She realizes she isn't the only one who is lost.

I found your cat.

Thank you!
She keeps getting out.

And just like that, it happens ...

It grows and grows, filling up her brain
until there is no more room for sad.

She races home and gets to work.

Her hands are happy to be building again.
And her assistant is happy to be assisting again.

But no one is more pleased by her idea than those who inspired it.

The next morning, her idea machine is running at top speed.

She might not have new ideas every day, but she trusts that they will happen eventually.

Some of those ideas will be good. Some of them will be great.
But each day that she gets to make things will be MAGNIFICENT.